Diamond in the Sky

by Jerlene Cannon

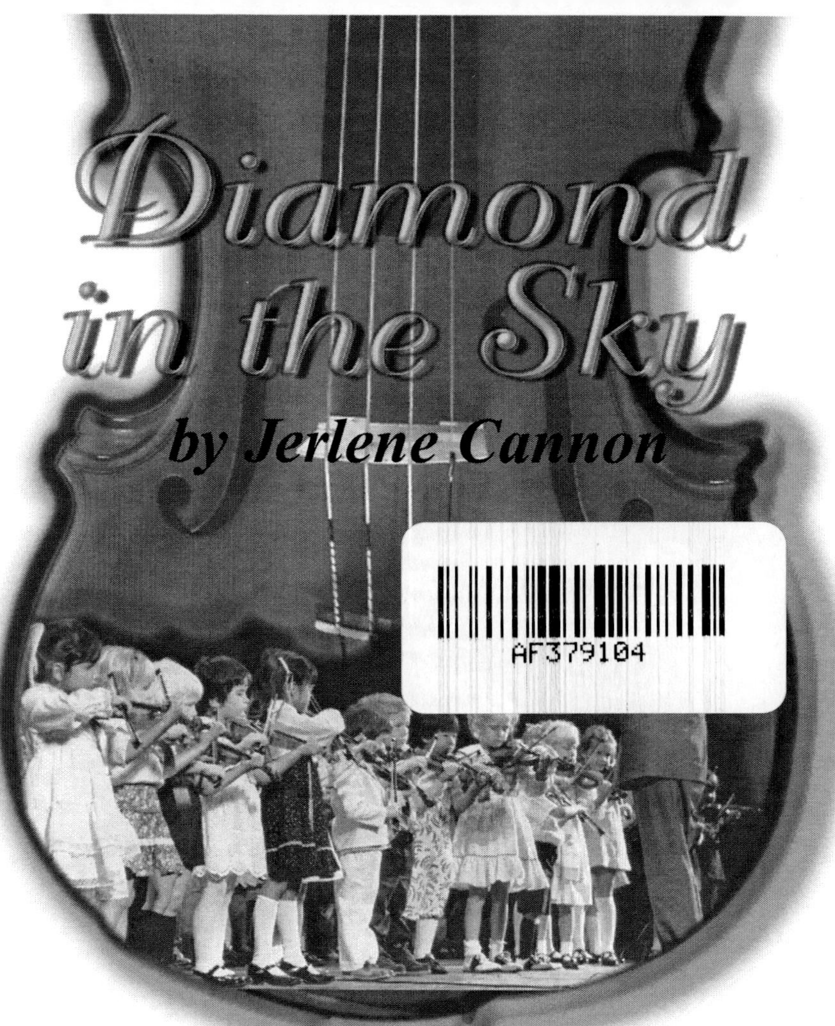

To Kathryn and Miss Maria

Art Design & Layout: Thais Yanes
Illustrations: Rama Hughes
Cover Photo: © Arthur Montzka

© 2002 Summy-Birchard Music
Division of Summy-Birchard Inc.
Exclusive print rights administered by
Alfred Publishing Co., Inc.
All Rights Reserved. Printed in USA

ISBN: 1-58951-40-9

Table of Contents

1.   A Boy in Nagoya 4

2.   A Special Gift 7

3.   An Expedition and Lifelong Friends 13

4.   Germany, a Teacher, and Romance 18

5.   A Bride for Shinichi 23

6.   A Musician and a Teacher 25

7.   War and Separation 29

8.   Triumph 33

Thank you, Miriam Rogers, for your great editing. Keith, this is your book too. To say thanks just doesn't cover it.

Preface

On March 27, 1955, 1,500 children gathered at the Tokyo Municipal Gymnasium in Sendagaya, Japan, to honor students who were graduating from a program called Talent Education. The special thing about these 1,500 children was this: They were all violinists studying under the direction and nurture of one man. That man was Shinichi Suzuki, and this is the story of his incredible quest to bring music into the hearts of children everywhere.

Chapter 1
A Boy in Nagoya

It was just after supper—and almost a hundred years ago—when a small boy slipped out the door and skipped down the path that led from his home to the nearby factory. The setting sun had turned the sky from red to a hazy purple, which deepened to a dark blue as the evening grew later. Occasionally the light breeze brought the sound of a voice or the laugh of another neighborhood child to his ears. But young Shinichi Suzuki was intent on getting to the factory. He did not stop for interruptions.

It didn't take him long to get there. Shinichi let himself inside and made his way to an area filled with workers. He could almost taste the smell of varnish and polish in the air. Oil lamps hung from the ceiling, giving light to the workers below. Shinichi greeted them as he found a comfortable place to sit. Then he patiently waited and watched, his eyes following the rough hands as workers polished the fronts and backs of violins until they shone in the lamplight.

Finally, one of the older men would begin a story. Shinichi listened intently—this was the reason he came to the factory every night. The storyteller would weave tales about the samurai, warriors who fought for their lords in long-ago Japan. These stories were terribly exciting to Shinichi. His own grandfather had been a samurai, the last in the Suzuki family to be one. So he listened to the story, breathless. Just at the most exciting part, the storyteller paused. Shinichi was jolted out of the past. This was his cue, as it was every night, to provide the storyteller with rice cakes. Shinichi jumped up and ran back to his home to fetch some from the kitchen. He knew that when he returned, the storyteller would finish the tale. So he hurried faster in the darkening night, swinging his imaginary sword at any samurai who might be lurking near.

Although Shinichi's grandfather really had been a samurai, the Suzuki family had another business enterprise. They made a musical instrument called a samisen. A samisen has three strings and looks sort of like a banjo. A pick is used to pluck the strings. Shinichi's great-grandfather had begun this instrument-making business. It had done well in the late 1800s in Japan. Shinichi's father, Masakichi, inherited the business in 1884 and he continued the tradition.

Masakichi was a very smart man. The family business changed from making samisens to making violins. Masakichi had heard someone playing a violin, and he loved the beautiful sound it made. He learned how to make one himself. It was actually the first one ever made in Japan, in 1888. Masakichi soon began to sell them. Eventually he built a factory in the city of Nagoya, where he could make a lot of violins at one time.

Ten years after Masakichi made that first violin, Shinichi was born October 17, 1898. By this time, the Suzuki Violin Factory was the largest one in the world. More than 1,000 people worked there. Masakichi always worked hard to learn the best way to make the violins using machines. When everything was working well, the factory could turn out 400 violins in one day.

Young Shinichi didn't really understand what a violin was or that each one had great value. He had never heard one played. He saw so many of them every day as they were being made in the factory. He must have thought they were common things instead of special musical instruments.

One day, Shinichi and his younger brother were playing at the factory and began play fighting. Before they knew it, they had become samurai warriors in a fierce fight, using two half-made violins for swords! They swung at each other as the battle raged. But when the two violins crashed against each other, they clattered to the ground in pieces. The boys stared down at them. Their older brother had heard the fighting. When he came into the room, Shinichi's heart began pounding. But his brother only picked up the broken violins and left again without saying a word.

Shinichi felt so awful! Maybe he remembered all the times he had watched the workers polishing the violins with such care. Now he had caused two of them to break. He told himself that he would never fight again.

Chapter 2
A Special Gift

hinichi loved the violin factory and all the activity that went on there. He couldn't wait until he was old enough to be able to work there. Masakichi had bigger plans for his son. He wanted Shinichi to take over the family business after he was grown. So when Shinichi was about 14 years old, he went to the Nagoya Commercial School to study how to operate a business. You may think of this as high school. The year Shinichi entered the school was 1912, a time of change for Japan. The emperor had died and his son, Hirohito, became Japan's new ruler.

At the commercial school, Shinichi learned how to run a business. It took him four years to finish. The school had a motto: First character, then ability. That meant Shinichi was expected to develop good qualities in himself, such as honesty, kindness, goodness, patience, and discipline. *Then,* using his good character, Shinichi could put into practice all the things he learned about running a business. Shinichi always tried his best to live by this motto.

Shinichi got good grades every year, but he didn't really like the schoolwork. He did enjoy sports, though. In fact, he was the pitcher on the school's baseball team. He could always throw the ball exactly where he wanted it to go. His classmates really liked him. They elected him president of the class all four years that he was in school. During the summers when Shinichi was not in school, he worked at the factory.

About halfway through Shinichi's high school years, Japan declared war on Germany and entered World War I. It was this same year, when Shinichi was 16 years old, that he was challenged by the school bully. All the students had come in to change their shoes after playing outside. Shinichi was putting on his shoes when the bully came up to him. This guy was strong and a good fighter. He did not like Shinichi, mostly because everyone else did. Shinichi knew trouble was coming. He tried to stay calm as he placed his outdoor shoes where they belonged on a rack.

The bully demanded that Shinichi put his shoes on the shoe rack too. Shinichi ignored him. This angered the bully, who demanded again, "Suzuki, didn't you hear me? Put away my shoes!"

Suzuki quietly answered, "Put away what is yours yourself."

The bully became furious at this comment and raised his fist to hit Shinichi. Shinichi was determined not to be a coward. He might get beaten up, but he wasn't going to run. He charged at the bully, thinking, *It's okay if I die.* He hit the bully right smack in the chest, knocking him over. The bully sprang up, surprised and enraged that Shinichi had not run away. He came at Shinichi again with both fists raised to strike. Shinichi charged again and knocked the bully down again. Just then someone pulled the two apart, and the fight was over. Shinichi's classmates were glad that Shinichi had the courage to face down the bully—he wasn't so mean after that!

On the way home from school each day, Shinichi usually stopped at the factory. One day—he was 17 years old now—he discovered an English typewriter in the office. Shinichi had never seen one before. He couldn't resist pressing the keys. An office manager came in and noticed what Shinichi was doing. "You mustn't type without paper in the machine," he told him.

Shinichi quickly responded, "Oh, but I wasn't really pressing down on the keys."

The man nodded and went out. Shinichi was left alone in the quiet office. He could feel his face grow hot as he felt shame that he had told a lie. And he had told it so quickly instead of just saying he was sorry. Why did the lie come to him so easily? Shinichi jumped up and headed for home.

Being at home didn't make him feel any better. He was so angry with himself for being dishonest. Too restless to sit at home, he went out for a walk. He roamed the streets of Nagoya and ended up going into a bookstore. As he browsed among the books, he randomly selected one from the shelf. It was a copy of *Tolstoy's Dairy.* He opened the book and read these words: "To deceive oneself is worse than to deceive others."

Shinichi was shocked. It was as if this line had been written just for him. He bought the book and rushed home to read it. He ended up reading the book several times and became a big fan of the author. Shinichi found teachings that he would use for the rest of his life. He had developed a pattern of learning from his mistakes and then not repeating them.

About the time Shinichi was to graduate from school, Masakichi bought a special present for him. It was a record player called a gramophone. Today instead of using gramophones, we use CD players. This was a unique gift, and not very many families owned one at that time.

Shinichi was so excited that he went to a store as soon as he could. He wanted to buy a record for the gramophone. He decided on a song called *Ave Maria,* written by Schubert. Misha Elman played the song on the violin. Shinichi rushed back home to play the record.

Eagerly, Shinichi placed the record on the gramophone. He couldn't wait to hear it! As the music began, Shinichi grew very still. His excitement turned to awe as he listened to the beautiful tones the violin made. You may wonder how someone who saw violins every day wouldn't know how one sounded. There may be a couple of reasons why Shinichi was surprised. Maybe he had never heard anyone play the violin skillfully. Or perhaps he had not heard Western music until now, and *Ave Maria* was a new sound to his ears. Either way, Shinichi was amazed that it was coming from a violin. Wasn't this the very same instrument he had watched people make all of his life and had once used as a sword? He had no idea such beauty and tone could come from the instrument.

Suddenly, it was as if Shinichi had never seen a violin before. Now he wanted to know all about them. He wanted to *play* one! He took the familiar path to the factory. Once there, he made his way to where the finished violins were. He gazed at them, all newly polished and shining. Shinichi felt as if they had been keeping a secret from him all this time. Carefully he chose one and packed it up to take home. He couldn't wait to make the same clear sounds he had heard Misha Elman make.

Well, it was awful. Shinichi couldn't make his fingers move on the strings the way he wanted them to. And the strings even made his fingers hurt a little. The bow made terrible, scratchy sounds. He didn't know how to hold it. He didn't hear anything *close* to the sounds he'd heard on his record. He was frustrated, but he knew the secret was not in the violin but in the player. So he did not quit.

Instead, he returned to the record store. He would try a different song. He found one called *Haydn's Minuet,* also played by Misha Elman. He may have thought this one would be a little easier for a first-time player.

Shinichi's house was filled with the sound of the minuet. He played the record over and over. His brothers and sisters heard it as they got ready for their morning walk. The maids heard it as they did their work. His parents heard it as they sent everyone off to school and work. They all heard it in the evenings after dinner. Finally, Shinichi had it memorized. They breathed a sigh of relief—until they heard Shinichi trying to play it on his violin!

His violin still screeched and scratched. But now he knew the sound he wanted to make, and he knew what to do. He just had to practice until he got it right. So practice he did, every chance he got. His fingers hurt as they got used to the strings. His bow hand ached from holding it in the same position for so long. But he knew these things would go away the more he practiced, so he kept on. Finally, after one month, he could play *Haydn's Minuet* himself.

Meanwhile, the day that he had been looking forward to for four years finally came. Graduation! Shinichi was 18 years old when he finished his studies at Nagoya Commercial School. He began working at the factory full time. Bookkeeping was his main job. He kept track of the money that the factory earned and how much was spent making the violins. He also learned other jobs in the factory, such as how the violins were actually made and how they were sold.

He always did a good job, and the factory workers liked him. Even though his father owned the factory, Shinichi worked as hard as any of the employees. He arrived at work early and stayed late.

Shinichi's days were busy, and he was happy. Every morning at dawn, he and his younger brothers and sisters would walk to a nearby pond. They loved to feed the fish there. As soon as the family returned home, they had breakfast together. Then Shinichi left for the factory and worked until evening.

On Shinichi's walk home from work, the neighborhood children would rush to meet him. Holding his hands or hanging onto his legs, the kids walked him home. They laughed and talked and played on the way. Shinichi had a special love for children. They always had such fun together. He thrilled the children by giving them special attention, and in turn they loved and respected him.

The time he spent with children gave him the chance to watch how they played with each other, how they learned, how they were so trusting. Shinichi wondered at their innocence and thought that their souls must be things of beauty. He began to realize that as these children grew up, they would lose those qualities that are so special in small children. *Why?* he wondered. He decided that the way those children were educated must cause their loss of innocence and take away their natural curiosity that makes early learning quick and fun. These thoughts held and took root in his mind. They would later form the basis of his teaching method called Talent Education.

Chapter 3
An Expedition and Lifelong Friends

Shinichi's life settled into a routine. He was learning everything he possibly could at the factory. In the evenings he listened to his music and continued to practice his violin. While his life was routine, the world around him was in the height of World War I. Japan was successful in the war and won many important battles. It was during this wartime that Shinichi learned he had his own personal battle to fight.

Shinichi was 20 years old. For two days in a row he had felt sick during the afternoon and had to go home early and go to bed. On the third day he went to see a doctor, who had disturbing news. Shinichi had capillary bronchitis, a respiratory illness. In those days—the year was 1918—there was no cure or medicine that would make him well again. People did not always recover from bronchitis. Rest and a change of climate were the only things that would help.

Shinichi was very upset by this news. He dreaded going home and breaking this news to his father. His father would be concerned for Shinichi's health. Also, Shinichi knew his father needed him at the factory.

Shinichi sat down that evening with his father and told him what the doctor had said. Masakichi listened quietly. Then he calmly told Shinichi he would send him to an inn or hotel on the coast to recover. Somehow they would just have to manage at the factory. This would be hard on the family business, but Shinichi's health was more important. Shinichi was thankful and relieved and went to pack for his trip. The next day he took care of a few things at the factory. Then he left for the coast to stay at a place called Okitsu.

Shinichi woke to the sound of waves breaking gently on the beach. He got up and began a routine he would follow for the next three months. He slipped out of his room and walked down to the beach. As the sun rose higher in the sky, he strolled along the shoreline. He paused to pick up seashells and took deep breaths of the salty sea air. During the day he rested. In the evenings he returned to the beach.

It was a beautiful fall season. On sunny, warm days Shinichi loved to gaze at the sea. It was so clear and blue! During stormy days, he was captivated by the enormous gray waves that rushed onto the beach with a deafening crash, bursting into white foam.

During this time, Shinichi met a family staying at the same inn—Ichiro Yanagida and his wife and their two young children. They all became instant friends. They began taking their walks on the beach together. After a storm, Shinichi and the children would walk along the water's edge looking for conch shells. They held the shells to their ears, listening to the call of the sea.

Shinichi began to feel much better. After only three months, he returned home to Nagoya. He went to the doctor for a checkup. His doctor said Shinichi's health had improved but that he should not return to work right away.

In early summer of that year—it was 1919 and Shinichi was 21 years old—Shinichi received a letter from Mr. Yanagida. He was planning to join an expedition, a group of people sailing to some islands to do biology research there. The Marquis Yoshichika Tokugawa, a Japanese nobleman who lived in Tokyo, would lead the expedition. Mr. Yanagida invited Shinichi to join them.

Shinichi's father approved of the trip. He thought that being out at sea would help Shinichi continue to recover. So in August 1919, Shinichi set sail on a new adventure.

The expedition was wonderful and full of new things for Shinichi. The weather was beautiful. Shinichi spent his days at sea out in the bright sunlight. Sometimes he could see whales or porpoises in the clear water. He spent time with the biologists as they went about their work. And of course he practiced on his violin. A pianist was on board, Miss Nobu Koda. In the evenings the whole group enjoyed listening to their music as they played together.

Sometimes he went along with the researchers as they did their work on the islands, collecting samples of plants. One day as they walked along the beach, a researcher glanced up and noticed some unusual moss clinging to the cliff face. He wished he could get some of it but didn't know how to reach it. Shinichi told the researcher he was sure he could get it. His feet kicked up sand as he ran ahead. His plan was to climb up the cliff from the beach.

As he got closer, Shinichi realized the moss was much higher than it had looked from a distance. There was no way he could climb that high up the cliff! He couldn't back out, though. He asked for a scoop, a small garden tool, to throw at the moss. He thought maybe he could knock it down. He took careful aim and threw the scoop. It landed right in the middle of the moss and held firm. *That* wasn't what he wanted! Everyone was watching him expectantly, wondering what he would do next.

Well, he didn't want to embarrass himself, but he had promised the moss and he wanted to deliver it. So he grabbed a rock and aimed this time for the scoop. His friends thought this was all part of the plan, but inwardly he was nervous. What if he *missed*?

The rock struck the scoop handle so hard that both the scoop and the moss fell down to the beach. Shinichi breathed a huge sigh of relief as his friends cheered.

Shinichi's constant violin practice was paying off. The music he and Ms. Koda played each evening was beautiful. Mr. Tokugawa especially enjoyed Shinichi's playing. Toward the end of the cruise, he suggested that Shinichi study music instead of going back to work in his father's factory. But Shinichi knew his father expected him to return to work as soon as he was able. Besides, Shinichi enjoyed working at the factory. He continued to play the violin because he was interested in music as art. He had not thought of actually studying to play better.

After the cruise was over, Mr. Tokugawa visited the Suzuki family. During the visit, he made the same suggestion to Mr. Suzuki that Shinichi should study music. Masakichi must have had great respect for Mr. Tokugawa because he agreed to let Shinichi study music.

So at the age of 21, Shinichi left Nagoya for Tokyo. He took violin lessons from KoAndo, who was Miss Koda's little sister. He also studied music theory and acoustics. During his stay in Tokyo, he lived with Mr. Tokugawa's family in their beautiful mansion.

Chapter 4
Germany, a Teacher, and Romance

$\mathcal{S}$hinichi was a young man now, studying violin and music in Tokyo. When he was 22 years old, Mr. Tokugawa invited him to go on a world tour. It was 1920 and World War I was over. Mr. Tokugawa's offer was tempting, but Shinichi believed he should not interrupt his music studies. So he said no.

On his next visit home, Shinichi mentioned the trip to his father. Surprisingly, his father wanted him to go because it was a great opportunity to see the world. His father also knew that Mr. Tokugawa would look after Shinichi. Masakichi even offered to give Shinichi extra money for the trip.

Still Shinichi refused. He was dedicated to the idea of studying music. He believed he had not been studying long enough to take a break from it. When he returned to Tokyo, Shinichi mentioned to Mr. Tokugawa that his father had wanted him to go on the tour and had offered to pay for it. This news caused Mr. Tokugawa to think of the perfect solution.

Mr. Tokugawa's suggestion was that Shinichi should accept his father's offer of money and begin the tour. When they reached Germany, Shinichi should try to stay there and find a good violin teacher. If this plan worked, Shinichi could use his father's money for living expenses.

When the 23-year-old Shinichi arrived in Germany, he found a place very different from Japan. Germany's defeat in World War I left the country in very bad condition. Many people were out of work. There was hardly enough food for everyone. German money (the mark) was not worth very much. While the mark wouldn't buy much, Shinichi's Japanese money (the yen) was worth a lot and he could live cheaply there.

When Shinichi reached Berlin, Germany's capital city, he rented a hotel room. His plan was to go to as many concerts as possible. He wanted to find a musician who played well and beautifully and who could help Shinichi better himself as a violinist.

After three months of searching, Shinichi had found no one. He was about to give up the search when he went one night to hear the Klingler Quartet. Their music was beautiful. Shinichi saw that they used excellent techniques as they played. He believed that the leader of the quartet, Karl Klingler, was the one who could teach him. The morning after the concert, Shinichi sent a request to him. He asked Professor Klingler to be his teacher. Shinichi was very happy when the professor invited him to come play for him.

Shinichi practiced and practiced, preparing the piece he would play for Klingler. Finally, the day came when he played for the professor at his home. As he played, Shinichi messed up in a couple of places. He thought this would make the great violinist reject him. After Shinichi finished, Klingler simply asked, "When can you come again?" Shinichi had found his teacher.

Shinichi's lessons each week were two hours long. Professor Klingler gave him many pieces to work on each week. Shinichi practiced them every day. Professor Klingler also taught Shinichi to play from his heart and make each piece beautiful to hear.

Now that Shinichi had a teacher, he would stay in Berlin. He rented a room in a woman's house. The woman could not hear well, so Shinichi could practice as loudly as he wanted! Now that he lived in a house with other people, Shinichi learned more quickly about the German way of life. He also had more chances to practice speaking German. Gradually he learned to speak the language well.

Shinichi was about 23 years old now, and once again his life settled into a routine. He had lessons with Professor Klingler once a week. In the evenings he went out to concerts or listened to concerts in the homes of good friends. He always listened to the very best music. He believed this would help him play his own violin better.

Shinichi chose good friends as well as good music. All of his friends were kind, good people. One such friend was Dr. Michaelis, whom Shinichi had met back in Nagoya. Since Shinichi was a foreigner living in Germany, Dr. Michaelis looked after Shinichi. He made sure Shinichi was doing well and did not get lonely. He introduced Shinichi to his friends. One evening, however, Dr. Michaelis told Shinichi that he would be moving. He told Shinichi not to worry, though. He had asked a friend of his to take care of Shinichi in his place.

That friend was Albert Einstein, the famous scientist. At first Shinichi was a little afraid of this great man, but Dr. Einstein was very kind. They discovered that they shared a love of music and the violin. The two quickly became good friends and often attended concerts together.

Every day Shinichi practiced for five hours. For a while he thought he was not getting better. When he listened to the great musicians of the Berlin Philharmonic Orchestra, he only felt worse—they could play so *well*. He thought they must have talent and he did not have any.

Shinichi thought that there was some secret to the art of music. He thought if he could find out that secret, it would make him a better person. If he were a better person, then he would be a better musician. So, he continued to study. He tried to learn more about the art of music. He stopped worrying so much that he had no talent. He began to play better. In fact, the more he searched for the beauty and secret of *art*, the better his ability to play the violin became.

All of these thoughts and experiences came together to teach Shinichi that man is a product of his environment. So, *how* a person is educated is extremely important. Shinichi believed that anyone could train him- or herself as long as the right kind of method was used. In his book, *Nurtured by Love,* he put it this way: "We have to train and educate our ability, that is to say, do the thing over and over again until it feels natural, simple, and easy. That is the secret."

When Shinichi was about 24 years old, he met a girl named Waltraud Prange at a home concert. She was 17, very beautiful, and she loved music. She had grown up in a loving home with her mother, one sister, and one brother. Her father had died when she was 11 years old. Waltraud and Shinichi became instant friends.

When Shinichi was 26 years old, he made a trip back home to see his family. He had been gone four years. Shinichi believed he could still learn more from Professor Klingler. He begged his father to let him return to Germany. It was actually a younger brother's turn to go study in another country. That brother agreed that Shinichi should return to Germany to finish what he had started. It was very kind of his brother to give up his turn. Shinichi must have been grateful.

When Shinichi returned to Germany, he continued his friendship with Miss Prange. She sang in a Catholic church choir and played the piano. Shinichi often played the violin while Waltraud accompanied him on the piano. Their friendship eventually grew into romance.

Shinichi and Waltraud knew things might not be easy for them if they got married. They were from two very different countries. Everything about the two of them was different: their manners, customs, language. Their friends and families loved both of them but were afraid these differences would be too much. However, the two young people remained committed to each other. Eventually they did get married.

Chapter 5
A Bride for Shinichi

Shinichi was 30 years old now, and his bride was 23. February 28, 1928, was a beautiful day. For their wedding, the couple followed German tradition. Instead of meeting at the church or not seeing each other until the actual ceremony, Shinichi took Waltraud from her home and escorted her to the church.

Shinichi arrived at Waltraud's home in a shining black carriage pulled by white horses. Inside, the carriage was as white as snow. Two coachmen attended the carriage—one drove in front and the other rode in back of the carriage on a footboard. Shinichi went to the door for Waltraud, led her back to the carriage, and seated her inside. He looked handsome in his black suit. Waltraud was a beautiful bride, dressed in a white dress and wearing a long white veil. They settled in for the ride to the church.

The church bells were ringing as they arrived. All of their family and friends were waiting. The couple stepped down from the carriage right onto red carpet. Two children walked in front of them, throwing flowers along the path. Shinichi and Waltraud followed the red carpet into the church and up to the altar. As they entered the church, the organist began playing a wedding march. The church choir sang during the ceremony. It was a wonderful wedding.

As the couple left the altar, a violinist played *Ave Maria*. They could hear the music as they followed the red carpet back down the aisle to the waiting carriage outside.

The love and friendship between Shinichi and Waltraud lasted as time went by. They did have differences because of their different cultures. Waltraud suffered homesickness when she moved to Japan, a country very foreign to her. Another war broke out and caused hard times for them. During that time they were brave, and their commitment to each other helped them. Waltraud believed in Shinichi and did all she could to help him reach his goals with music.

As the couple drove away in the bridal carriage, they did not know all of these things. But they did believe that no matter what happened, they would face it together.

Chapter 6
A Musician and a Teacher

ot long after Shinichi and Waltraud married, Shinichi's mother became very ill. The Suzukis decided to return to Nagoya. Except for a brief visit home four years earlier, Shinichi had been gone for eight years. His studies with Professor Klingler were over.

The Suzukis began their long trip back to Nagoya, Japan. They traveled mostly by train, and the trip was very long and tiring. Finally they arrived at the Nagoya station. The entire Suzuki household was there to welcome them home. Only Shinichi's father had stayed home to tend to his wife. How excited the family must have been that Shinichi had finally returned, and with a wife as well!

When Shinichi had gone to Berlin, he had been a foreigner in a strange city. But because that city was so large, there were many foreigners. It was not so unusual for a Japanese person to be seen in a German city. However, the same was not true for Waltraud. She was German, and foreigners were very unusual in Nagoya, Japan. So unusual, in fact, that the Suzuki family was not the only group at the station to greet Shinichi and Waltraud. Reporters were there also. This was a little scary to Waltraud. During the entire time that the couple lived in Nagoya, this did not change. She could never go anywhere without being stared at, talked about, or photographed. It became such a bother that she stayed at home most of the time.

During this time, a worldwide depression began. You may know of this as the stock market crash of 1929. Money lost its value, and many businesses had to close. Thousands of people were without jobs, so people became very poor. Masakichi Suzuki lost a great deal of money in the stock market crash. And because people were not buying violins, the factory could not make as many as it once had. Masakichi tried as long as he could to keep his workers. Eventually, though, he had to let most of them go because there was not enough work to do. The factory work moved to a smaller building.

Around this time Shinichi and Waltraud decided to move to Tokyo, which was a much larger city than Nagoya. They believed this would be easier for Waltraud. There were more foreigners in Tokyo and she could blend in better. They were very poor. Shinichi's father sent them enough money for living expenses, but Waltraud did not like this. She informed Shinichi that *he* needed to be the moneymaker for himself and his wife!

Perhaps this is what inspired Shinichi to organize a string quartet with three of his brothers. It was also a normal response to all of his training with Professor Klingler—it was only natural to do what his teacher had done. The Suzuki Quartet became a success. Once a week they played classical music on the radio. They began to travel, giving recitals from northern to southern Japan. The brothers worked well together and had fun together. When they weren't giving recitals, they were rehearsing for them.

Sometime in 1930, a father brought his son to Shinichi and asked the violinist if he would tutor the boy. Toshiya Eto was four years old. Shinichi asked for time to consider the request. How could he teach such a young child to play the violin? He thought and thought about it. Then the idea struck him—of course a child could learn to play an instrument. The secret would be in the *way* the child was taught.

Shinichi took this idea from the way a child learns to speak. By the time a child is two to three years old, he can speak fluently in his own language. Shinichi remembered when he was in Berlin struggling to learn the German language. He was amazed that very young children could speak it very well while he, an adult, worked so hard to learn it. The reason a child can speak his own language is because he hears it repeatedly from the day he is born and begins imitating it as soon as he is able. Through this method, his ability naturally gets better each day. *A child could learn to play the violin the same way!* Shinichi wrote many years later in *Nurtured by Love* that this idea hit him like a flash of light in a dark night.

Shinichi contacted Toshiya Eto's father and agreed to tutor the boy. Almost immediately after that, another parent brought a three-year-old boy named Koji Toyoda. Both of these young boys would grow up to be wonderful violinists through Shinichi's care and thoughtful teaching.

Word spread about Shinichi's efforts to teach young children. Soon other children came. Shinichi began working on music books that would help the children learn violin techniques step by step. Each step was harder than the last. Shinichi wrote ten of these books. It took him ten years to complete them. These are the same books that Suzuki students use today.

In 1931, when Shinichi was 33 years old, he started the Imperial Music School in Tokyo. He believed this was the best way to teach his own philosophy and methods. In addition to violin, the school offered voice, theory, and cello classes.

Now Suzuki was doing what he had dreamed of doing for so long—teaching children to develop art through music. He loved his work and worked very hard at it. He was able to do this work through most of the 1930s, but another great war was brewing. This war would interrupt his work and his life with Waltraud for a long time.

Chapter 7
War and Separation

*I*magine a beautiful mountain range sloping down to its foothills. In those foothills, picture a small town situated along river rapids that tumble down out of the mountains. It is early morning—the last star has just disappeared into the dawn. A man leaves his small house and walks briskly to a central point in the village, his breath making puffs of vapor in the chilly air. He stops, lifts an instrument to his shoulder, and suddenly fills the quiet morning with beautiful music. The man is Shinichi, playing his violin as he does each morning for the people of Kiso-Fukushima. He plays from his heart, trying to remind these mountain people that all is not lost in the hardships of war.

A second world war had begun in 1939. Most major countries of the world were fighting in it. Japan became actively involved in World War II in 1941, when Shinichi was about 43 years old. It had become hard to run the school. With a war going on, no one was interested in studying music. Eventually, Shinichi and the other teachers decided to close the school. It had been open for about ten years. They sold everything in the school, things such as furniture and equipment. They took the small amount of money and divided it among themselves. Shinichi, in his usual generous way, would not take any money. Instead he divided his share among the other teachers.

The Suzukis had another hard decision to make. Tokyo was the target of air raids, and every day they grew worse. Shinichi and Waltraud knew they needed to leave the city. The big question was where should they go? They had to consider Waltraud's safety because she was a foreigner. Even though she was by marriage a Japanese citizen, during this time of war foreigners were looked upon with suspicion. It was a time of fear, and no one trusted foreigners.

Shinichi had also learned that his father needed help. The Japanese government had ordered the factory in Nagoya to stop making violins. Instead, the workers were making floats for seaplanes that were used in the war. Masakichi had enough workers and equipment but not enough supplies. The wood needed to make the floats came from forest property Masakichi owned up in the Kiso-Fukushima mountains. He needed someone to go there and be in charge of cutting the trees down and shipping them to Nagoya.

Shinichi volunteered to help his father, but he had to go to the mountains alone. It would not be safe for Waltraud to go with him. Instead, she moved to their small vacation house in Hakone. Hakone was one of two villages where foreigners were being sent to live during the war. Leaving each other was very hard for Waltraud and Shinichi. They had been married for 13 years now. However, they did not think the war would last much longer. They hoped they would be together again soon.

The villagers of Kiso-Fukushima must have been glad for the chance to work. There was a factory there, and Shinichi converted it to a lumber factory. Every day they cut down trees and sawed the timber so that they could ship it to Nagoya. Shinichi didn't know anything about a lumber factory. He had to learn each part of this process. His father had taught him always to make the best of any situation, so he dedicated himself to doing as best he could.

The war dragged on. With each year, life became harder. Shinichi's sister's husband died, and she and her children came to live with Shinichi. Although the mountains were beautiful, the winters were terribly cold and miserable. Food became scarce. Sometimes Shinichi's family had to eat the moss that grew on rocks in the river to keep from starving.

Whenever he could, Shinichi traveled to Hakone to see Waltraud. She was bravely enduring the war alone. The Japanese people did not trust her because she was a foreigner. Her fellow foreigners did not trust her because she was married to a Japanese. She was always so happy and relieved to see Shinichi.

Finally in 1945 the war ended. Japan was in a shambles and had been made poor by the war. In Kiso-Fukushima, Shinichi decided to stop the factory work for a while. No one knew what was happening or how life would continue now that the war was over. All was quiet in the village. At night, Shinichi would stare up at the stars, wondering how Japan could recover from being torn apart. He always thought of the children and how healing should begin with them. He believed that rebuilding could begin if the nation's children were looked after and given a good education. Shinichi would spend the rest of his life trying to make that happen.

Chapter 8
Triumph

One day in Kiso-Fukushima, Shinichi had a visitor. Kuniji Kajikura was a journalist with *Central Japan Newspaper.* Kajikura came with news from a group of people in Matsumoto, Japan. They wanted to start a music school, and they wanted Shinichi's help. One of the people in the group was a voice teacher who had taught at the Imperial Music School.

Shinichi had a ready answer. This was exactly what he had been thinking of during his quiet times in the mountain village. He did not want to work with people who already knew how to play. He had worked out a new method he wanted to teach to small children. He wanted to teach children to develop ability. He had begun this work at the Imperial Music School and had been doing research on this idea for many years. He would help with a new school now, but only if he could teach based on his research and focus on children.

Everyone agreed with Shinichi. The Matsumoto group wanted him to begin right away. At first, Shinichi traveled to Matsumoto once a week. This became too much, and he soon moved there. His wife had begun working for the American Red Cross at the end of the war and now had a job in Tokyo. Because he was starting a new job, they needed her income to pay living expenses. So he was alone once more and threw himself into developing the new school.

This is when Talent Education really began. Shinichi was 47 years old. It seemed that everything he had done in his life had prepared him for this time. The school immediately began to grow as Shinichi proved that children could develop musical abilities rather than hope they had talent. In a very caring way, Shinichi taught the children to imitate his violin movements, or techniques, and to repeat them over and over until they were perfect. The new school in Matsumoto was going to succeed.

Before long, Shinichi knew he had to fight another battle of his own. Japan was barely recovering from the war, and the people of the country were given food rations. During this time, Shinichi started feeling a little ill. He thought it was because of the food rations—they didn't get very much to eat. And Shinichi had always had a very weak stomach anyway. But he kept getting more and more sick. Soon he couldn't even get out of bed. He sent for his sister to come help him. Waltraud was very upset and worried about Shinichi, but she was the only one able to work and earn money for the family. She had to stay in Tokyo. She traveled to Matsumoto each weekend to help care for Shinichi.

Finally, a new doctor and a new diet helped Shinichi recover. A month after he began his new diet, he was able to take a walk.

During his long recovery, Shinichi worked on a new way for children to learn addition and subtraction math facts. Apparently, school children memorized only multiplication and division tables. Shinichi believed that addition and subtraction facts could and should be memorized also and would improve a child's math skills. As Shinichi's sister listened to him recite math facts over and over as he lay in his bed, she was afraid he had lost his mind. (Some elementary schools did adopt this method in later years.)

As soon as Shinichi was completely well, he again devoted all of his time to the Talent Education program. He traveled throughout Japan to give lectures about it. From the time it began in 1945, it kept growing. Other groups who learned Shinichi's methods sprang up in different places outside Matsumoto. In 1950 the school became incorporated when it was registered with the Ministry of Education in Japan.

Shinichi's way of teaching young children spread rapidly. After the war, as people tried to rebuild their lives, many were thankful that their children could be involved in this new way of learning. As more and more children learned to play, the program became even more popular. When Shinichi first started, he held classes in his home. Eventually he had to move to a bigger home where a Western-style room was built on. Music sounded much better in this new room. Finally, teachers and parents put their money together to construct a building especially for the school. They called it the Kaikan.

In 1953, just eight years after the school started, the first graduation was held. There were 195 graduates. The following year at the second graduation ceremony, there were 363 graduates. This was a time of triumph for Shinichi and all who were involved in Talent Education at the Matsumoto school. It was a rewarding time for the parents of the children who were attending the school. It was a time of learning and success for the young students. They were proof that Shinichi's methods of teaching were sound. These students provided encouragement to those who would come after them.

As usual, Shinichi wanted to give back to those who gave to him. So he suggested planning a concert to honor those who had graduated. All students enrolled in Talent Education were invited to participate. The concert was planned for March 1955. Preparations were made to use this concert as an opportunity for the rest of the world to learn about Talent Education.

The day of the grand national concert finally arrived. Because so many students were there, 1,500 of them, the concert was held at the Tokyo Municipal Gymnasium. What a moment that must have been for Shinichi, who was now 57 years old. The small stage sat in the center, where two grand pianos were placed to accompany the violins. The students circled the stage, each circle bigger than the one before it so that all 1,500 students faced the stage. From there, Shinichi could see all of them. As one person, they raised their violins to their shoulders, placed their bows on the strings, and began to play.

Epilogue

The first national concert provided an opportunity for Talent Education to spread outside of Japan. A film had been made that was eventually sent to Oberlin College in Ohio. This film was shown at the Ohio String Teachers Conference. Based on that film, observers began traveling to Japan to see firsthand how Talent Education worked. Talent Education soon became known as the "Suzuki Method."

Waltraud Suzuki, meanwhile, had worked in Tokyo many years to help pay for their new home in Matsumoto and the addition of the new room where Shinichi taught. When that was paid for, she finally quit her job and moved to Matsumoto in 1956. The couple had been living apart since 1941 when they were forced to separate because of the war. They had been apart for almost 15 years. During that time, their commitment to each other and to Shinichi's dream of Talent Education had never wavered.

In 1959 and again in 1962, John Kendall, who had seen the film of the grand national concert, visited Japan to observe Talent Education. He returned to the United States and held workshops all over the country. He asked Shinichi to travel to the United States.

In March of 1964, nine years after the first national concert, the Suzukis and a small group of parents and children left for the United States. They made stops across the country—Shinichi gave talks about how to nurture talent in small children. The children gave concerts as demonstrations. The tour was extremely successful. String teachers in colleges all over the country opened Talent Education programs for children. Since this first tour, the Suzukis were invited back to the United States each summer so that Shinichi could continue lecturing.

In June of 1966 the New England Conservatory in Boston awarded Shinichi with an honorary doctorate of music. Over the years, he received this honor from various universities. When he accepted that first degree, Shinichi smiled and said that honorary degrees are given to a person who does nothing. Though he made light of his accomplishments, to this day he is consistently and very affectionately referred to as "Dr. Suzuki."

In 1970 the Suzuki children made their first European tour. They stopped in Berlin, Germany; London, England; and Lisbon, Portugal. These tours were continued and eventually extended to include such countries as Peru and China.

In Japan, Talent Education outgrew its building. In the late 1970s, the Suzuki Institute building was completed. It was paid for by a private donor, David Smith. He was so impressed with the work described in Shinichi's book, *Nurtured by Love,* that he wanted to make a contribution.

Shinichi never stopped working toward his goal of educating all children everywhere. In 1984 the International Suzuki Association (ISA) was founded. This association is dedicated to preserving the teaching methods Shinichi developed. Associations have been formed all over the world and work with the ISA to continue Shinichi's work.

For the remainder of his life, Shinichi devoted his efforts to teaching children. Over time, other instruments were added to his instruction method: cello, piano, flute, and guitar. Every spring, students in Japan continue to play the national concert.

In 1998 Shinichi Suzuki died in his home in Matsumoto, Japan. He was 99 years old. It seems that in his lifetime, he never wasted a moment.

Resources

Nurtured by Love, Shinichi Suzuki, 1983, Summy-Birchard Inc.,
exclusively distributed by Warner Bros. Publications, Inc.
15800 NW 48th Avenue, Miami, Florida, 33014.

Shinichi Suzuki: Man of Love, Masaaki Honda, 1978, Zen-On Music
Company, Ltd. English-language edition 1984 by
Summy-Birchard Inc., exclusively distributed by
Warner Bros. Publications, Inc.
15800 NW 48th Avenue, Miami, Florida, 33014.

My Life with Suzuki, Waltraud Suzuki, 1987, Summy-Birchard Inc.,
exclusively distributed by Warner Bros. Publications, Inc.
15800 NW 48th Avenue, Miami, Florida, 33014.

Related Internet Sites

Suzuki Music Academy
http://www.suzukimusicacademy.com

American Suzuki Talent Education Center
http://finearts.uwsp.edu/suzuki

Suzuki Association of the Americas
http://www.suzukiassociation.org

Enter INTERNATIONAL SUZUKI ASSOCIATION as search words
in your Internet browser to access various links concerning that
association.

Photo: © Arthur Montzka